Teletubbies™

Laa-Laa's Ball

BBC CHILDREN'S BOOKS

One day in Teletubbyland,
Laa-Laa was playing with her ball.

La la la la la
boing!

Lalalalala
wobble
bobble

But then, Laa-Laa had an accident.

Uh-oh!

Accident!

Laa-Laa tried to reach the ball.

But Laa-Laa wasn't tall enough.

Dipsy came to help.

Dipsy was taller than Laa-Laa. But Dipsy wasn't tall enough to reach the ball.

Never mind.

Big hug!

Tinky Winky came to help.

Tinky Winky was the tallest Teletubby.
But Tinky Winky wasn't tall enough to
reach the ball.

Never mind.
Big hug!

Po came to help.

Po was the smallest Teletubby,

but Po thought she could reach the ball.

Po span round and round with the bag.

Po let go of the bag.

bonk!
ball!

At last Laa-Laa had her ball back.

Clever Po!

Teletubbies love each other very much.

Look out for the Teletubbies books, audio and video tapes.

First published in 1997 by BBC Children's Publishing, a division of BBC Worldwide Ltd
Woodlands, 80 Wood Lane, London W12 0TT

Adapted from the original script by Andrew Davenport
Illustrations by Lucy Su.

ISBN 0 563 38051 9

Printed in Great Britain by Cambus Litho Ltd.